Teeny Witch and the Perfect Valentine

by LIZ MATTHEWS
illustrated by CAROLYN LOH

Troll Associates

Library of Congress Cataloging-in-Publication Data

Matthews, Liz.
Teeny Witch and the perfect valentine / by Liz Matthews; illustrated by Carolyn Loh.
p. cm.
Summary: Teeny Witch tries hard to get perfect valentine gifts for her three aunts and succeeds when she thinks she has failed.
ISBN 0-8167-2280-3 (lib. bdg.) ISBN 0-8167-2281-1 (pbk.)
[1. Valentine's Day—Fiction. 2. Witches—Fiction. 3. Aunts—Fiction.] I. Loh, Carolyn, ill. II. Title.
PZ7.M4337Td 1991
[E]—dc20 90-11204

10 9 8 7 6 5 4 3

It was a cold, snowy day. Teeny Witch and her friend, Jenny, were walking home. They had been sleigh riding in the park. As they went through town, they looked in every store window they passed.

Suddenly, a gust of chilly wind made the two friends shiver.
"Brr! I hate February," Jenny said.
"I like February," said Teeny.
"February is a cold, windy month," said Jenny. "Why do you like it?"

"Valentine's Day is in February," said Teeny. "On Valentine's Day you show people how much you care for them."

Jenny smiled and nodded. Valentine's Day was only two days away. "I like Valentine's Day, too," Jenny said.

"What are you going to get your aunts for Valentine's Day?" Jenny asked.

Teeny thought about her three funny aunts. Sometimes they did some really silly things. But they always took very good care of Teeny. She loved them very much.

"I don't know," said Teeny. "I want to get them something extra special for Valentine's Day. I want to show them how much I care for them."

The girls started walking again. Jenny turned the corner by her house. Teeny walked on alone. She looked in the window of a candy store. Her eyes opened wide.

"That's it!" she shouted. "That's what I'll get my aunts for Valentine's Day."

There were boxes of candy in the window. In the middle of all the boxes were three special ones. They were very fancy. They were pink and shaped like hearts. And on each box was a bright red ribbon. Printed on the ribbon was the word "love."

"I will buy my aunts one of those special boxes of candy," said Teeny. She went into the store and asked about the special boxes.

"Each box is ten dollars," said the candy store man. "The candy is extra special. I only have three boxes left."

"Thank you," said Teeny. "I will go home and count my money. I hope I have ten dollars."

Teeny Witch rushed home.

Her aunts were waiting for her at home. They were surprised when Teeny zipped by them.

"Hi, Aunt Icky! Hi, Aunt Ticky! Hi, Aunt Vicky!" called Teeny as she zoomed past.

"Goodness," said Aunt Icky.

"Teeny is sure in a hurry," said Aunt Ticky.

"I wonder what the big rush is all about?" asked Aunt Vicky.

Lickety-split, Teeny ran upstairs to her room. She took out her piggy bank. She popped the plug out of the piggy's tummy. Plink! Money poured out. Teeny began to count. Did she have enough for the Valentine candy?

"Ickity-stick!" said Teeny. "I don't have enough money. And Valentine's Day is Saturday." Teeny thought for a minute. "But Saturday is also the day I get my allowance. On Saturday I will have enough money to buy the candy. Hooray!"

Teeny put her money back in the bank. "I hope no one buys those boxes of candy before Saturday," she said.

Just then, Teeny heard Aunt Icky call, "Teeny, time for dinner."

"Coming," Teeny called.

At dinner, Teeny talked about the holiday. She told her aunts how much she liked Valentine's Day.

"I like Halloween," said Aunt Icky.

"I like Christmas," said Aunt Ticky.

"I like National Ugly Bug Day," said silly Aunt Vicky.

That made Teeny shiver. She did not like bugs at all.

After dinner, Aunt Ticky and Aunt Vicky got up.
"Let's go watch our favorite TV show,"
said Aunt Ticky.

"Let's go, too," Teeny Witch said to Aunt Icky.
"I can't," said Aunt Icky. "Aunt Vicky set the table. Aunt Ticky cooked the dinner. It is my job to wash the dirty dishes."

"I will help," said Teeny.
"But you will miss the TV show," said Aunt Icky.
"I will help anyway," said Teeny. "If we work together, we will finish faster. Then we can both watch part of the TV show."

Teeny and Aunt Icky did the dishes. The work went fast. Soon it was done. Then Teeny and Aunt Icky watched their favorite show.

The next day Teeny went to the park with Jenny. On the way home for lunch, Teeny stopped at the candy store. She looked in the window. What an awful surprise! There were only two fancy boxes of candy left.

"Oh no!" said Teeny. "Someone bought a box of candy. I hope no one buys the other two before Saturday."

LOVE
LOVE

While Teeny Witch was eating lunch, it started to snow. It snowed all afternoon. When the snow stopped, Teeny went out to play. She started to build a snowman. Then she heard someone huffing and puffing.

It was Aunt Ticky.

"Why are you huffing and puffing?" asked Teeny Witch.

"Shoveling snow is hard work," said Aunt Ticky. "And there is a lot to shovel."

Teeny Witch smiled. "My snowman can wait," she said. "I will help you."

Teeny Witch helped Aunt Ticky shovel snow. Soon all the snow was cleared away.

"Thank you," said Aunt Ticky. "You are a good little helper."

Later that day, Teeny Witch went back to the store to look at the two fancy boxes of candy. But now there weren't two fancy boxes of candy in the window.

"Ickity-stick!" said Teeny. "There is only one box left!"

Teeny Witch felt very sad. She thought about that box of candy all the way home. She wanted to buy it for her aunts. She wanted to show them how much she cared for them. Would that box of candy still be there on Saturday?

That night, Teeny tried to cheer herself up. She made valentines for her friends. She cut out pretty valentine hearts. She made an extra nice valentine for her friend Jenny.

Teeny was cutting out more valentines when she heard Aunt Vicky yell.

"EEK!" yelled Aunt Vicky. "I need help. My ugly bugs are getting away."

Zip! Teeny dashed into Aunt Vicky's room. "I dropped my bug box," Aunt Vicky said. "My bug collection is crawling away. Help me collect my bugs, Teeny."

Teeny shivered. She did not like bugs. But Aunt Vicky needed help. Bugs were crawling here. Bugs were crawling there. Bugs were crawling everywhere.

"I'll help you, Aunt Vicky," said Teeny.

Teeny crawled after bugs. Aunt Vicky crawled after bugs. Soon all the bugs were collected and back in the box.

"Thank you, Teeny," said Aunt Vicky. "I couldn't have done it without you."

The next morning, Teeny Witch dressed lickety-split. Zoom! She zipped downstairs. "Hooray! It's Valentine's Day!" she shouted.

"We know," said Aunt Icky. She smiled.

"Here is your allowance," said Aunt Ticky.

Teeny took her allowance. "Where is Aunt Vicky?" asked Teeny.

"She went out," said Aunt Ticky.

"She said something about a surprise," said Aunt Icky.

"Later, I'll have a surprise, too," said Teeny. "Now I have something to do." And she rushed off.

Teeny took the money out of her piggy bank. She added it to her allowance money. She finally had enough for the candy. Teeny rushed down to the candy store.

What an awful surprise! There were no fancy boxes of candy left.

"I am sorry," said the man. "I just sold the last box of candy. I have no more to sell."

Teeny Witch felt very sad. What could she do? She wanted to buy something for her aunts for Valentine's Day. She went to the flower shop. She bought a nice pink flower that had a red, heart-shaped balloon tied to it.

Teeny started for home. The cold February wind began to blow. It blew very hard.

Whoosh! Away blew the red, heart-shaped balloon.

"Oh no!" said Teeny.

Whoosh! The wind blew harder. Away blew the pink flower's petals. Teeny looked at her flower.

"What an awful Valentine gift," said Teeny Witch.

When Teeny got home, her three aunts were waiting. They looked at what was left of Teeny's flower.

"What is that?" they asked.

"It's your Valentine gift," said Teeny. "The cold wind blew away the flower's petals. It blew away the heart-shaped balloon." Teeny started to cry. "I wanted something special to show how much I care for you. But this gift is all I have."

Teeny's three witch aunts smiled.
"Every day is Valentine's Day here," said Aunt Icky.
"Every day you show us how much you care for us," said Aunt Ticky.
"How?" asked Teeny.
"You show us by helping us," said Aunt Vicky.
"Teeny Witch, *you* are our special gift."

Teeny Witch stopped crying. She felt very happy.

LOVE
LOVE

The three witch aunts took out their gifts. The gifts were three boxes of candy. The boxes were all very fancy. They were pink and shaped like hearts. On each box was a bright red ribbon. Printed on each was the word "love."

"HOORAY!" shouted Teeny. "Valentine's Day is a very special holiday."

And she gave each one of her aunts a very, very big hug.